Edwin John Ellis

The Greymare Romance

Edwin John Ellis

The Greymare Romance

ISBN/EAN: 9783337345044

Printed in Europe, USA, Canada, Australia, Japan

Cover: Foto ©Andreas Hilbeck / pixelio.de

More available books at **www.hansebooks.com**

THE

GREYMARE ROMANCE.

BY

EDWIN J. ELLIS.

*WITH TITLE-PAGE AND TWENTY-FOUR ILLUSTRATIONS
BY THE AUTHOR.*

GEORGE ALLEN,
8, BELL YARD, TEMPLE BAR, LONDON;
AND
SUNNYSIDE, ORPINGTON.
1891.

LIST OF ILLUSTRATIONS.

LIST OF ILLUSTRATIONS.

THE GREYMARE ROMANCE.

———◆———

CHAPTER I.

" I DARESAY you think that as I am only a little donkey my opinion is not worth having," said a strange voice in my ear; adding, in an injured tone, "There, I knew it."

Between the first words and the last I had looked round for the speaker, and discovered that there was no human being visible. The time was near midnight. The place was Barnes Common. I was young, and unprosperously, though not quite hopelessly, in love. The weather was warm and cloudy. There

I

was no moon. I had come out to think, and was lying on my back doing so.

All of a sudden it flashed upon me that perhaps, in the darkness, a Thought Reader had come out with the same purpose, and had been distracted from his intention by the thread of my meditations, which I had been told that these gifted people could decipher from the mind-waves that roll out of the head as easily as a clerk can read the tape that crawls from a telegraphic machine.

I sat up and looked round.

"You are right enough so far," said the voice, "but your commonest phases of consciousness want cultivating. You do not even know what you think yourself."

"Yes, I do," I replied, out loud, at hazard ; for if one can do nothing else with a bodiless voice one can at least contradict it. "I was thinking, when you interrupted me, of the way in which her hair last night——"

" Before that," said the voice, with a quiet assumption of knowing all that I had thought about her hair last night.

" Well, let me see," I began, setting my wits to work in earnest ; " before that we were on the balcony, and her hand——"

" I hate hands," said the voice, interrupting again ; " before that, please."

" As you seem to know all about it," I replied, getting irritated at last, " perhaps you will tell me what you mean, and where you are buried."

" I am not buried," it answered.

" Don't talk nonsense," I replied, " you are. Even on this dark night I should see your legs against the sky if you were standing about here. It is my belief that you are either a ghost, or a bit of new duplex tele- graphy photophone, under the surface of the common, working up through the grass on account of the night dew having got through a crack of the insulators and established a connection with the sod I am lying on."

The voice laughed, a rather unpleasant laugh—laughs that indicate that we are fools are so often unpleasant—and answered,—

"Do you not recollect that as you flung yourself down you observed an outcast donkey, grazing alone in the darkness, and said to yourself, with what you thought would have looked rather well by daylight as a cynical smile, that you were the biggest ass of the two?"

It was a fact. And what was more, I began to perceive that I was conversing with the donkey himself, or, as I learned presently, herself.

"Have I got brain fever?" I exclaimed. At the same moment the probable results raced through my mind,—the discovery of a well-dressed young man delirious on Barnes Common, the identification, the paragraph in the papers, the feelings of Violet when she read it, my gradual recovery and restoration to health, her assiduous care of me—that was her pale face flitting by the bed side on which my eyes had first dwelt with dreamy consciousness of blessed repose when the desperate struggle with the dark monster was over, and youth and my iron constitution had triumphed—and when her cool hand was laid——

"There you go about hands again," said the little donkey, in an impatient voice; "I do so hate them—nasty pulpy silly things; and so cunning and treacherous, winding round sticks and harness, and all that, and worrying your life out—hands indeed! I've got none myself, I'm proud to say, and if I overlook it in you, it is only because you are unusually intelligent for a man, and so I am glad to think as little about your defects as possible. Now listen to me.

When, on the stroke of midnight, one of
your lot and one of mine are face to face
and alone, and a ray of lucidity reveals to
you that you are not quite what you thought
yourself in the way of superiority to us, we
are permitted for one hour to speak to you.
As for my knowing what you were thinking,
that is nothing. We can all do that. We
are naturally what you call 'thought readers,'
only we are not such donkeys as to say so.
We should be worked to death in the city if
we admitted it. Carts are bad enough ;—but
commerce ! "

At this word I thought for a moment that
she was going to bray, but she checked herself
and continued,—

"We have been fooling too long over this
explanation. I have a story to tell you of
myself and a friend, which may help you,
and I am willing to do it in return for your
moment of mental humility. So now, as

there are only about forty-five minutes left
before the opportunity is gone for ever,—for
it would be too much to expect of you that
you should ever be humble again after you
have talked with me,—you had better listen."

I sat up and listened, feeling my pulse
furtively, and trying to remember what I had
read about the symptoms, and how the next
developments were likely to show themselves.

The Donkey paused to collect itself for a
long blast of concentrated egotism, and then
began as they do on the stage, when two
chairs are placed in the middle of a drawing-
room, right in the draught from the folding
doors.   And this is what she said :—

CHAPTER II

" IT was on this common that we first met—— "

" Who first met ? " I asked.

" Young Mr. Colter and I."

" Then you are a lady, I' presume ? " I exclaimed, lifting my hat.

" Of course," she answered, quietly.

I did not presume to interrupt again, but I remember saying to myself in a confused sort of way, as I was putting my hat on again, " Why not? There is nothing essentially unsuited to a lady in being a —— " There it stopped. The mute politeness that regulates even our thoughts for us without our knowing it, when we are meditating about those to whom we look up, put a reverential blankness over my mind before the last word shaped itself consciously. Perhaps also I had a half remembrance that my thoughts were being read like a book, but that need not have troubled me. On reflection, I do not seriously suppose that even donkeys, gifted as they are, can talk about the romance of their lives, and perceive what other people think of them at the same time.

"You have heard," she continued, "an old proverb which says that 'the grey mare is the better horse,'—it is the motto of the family. Mrs. Greymare was his mother. I need hardly add that Mr. Greymare was his father—— "

"*Mr.* Greymare?" I muttered; "surely—— "

"It hardly sounds like a masculine name, does it?" said the little Donkey. "But that

does not matter. I assure you I am quite in
order,—and in grammar. Just to give you
an example from among yourselves. In your
own language you say Mr. Siddons, do not
you? Very well. It is the same thing. If
you were obliged to say 'The husband of
Mrs. Siddons' each time, life would be too
short."

"Quite so," I assented, for I began to re-
flect that if we argued every point, life, or
rather three-quarters of an hour of it, would
not be long enough for the interesting story
I was about to hear.

"Well," she began again, "where was I?
Oh, yes: on this common we met. How
changed it is! There was hardly a house in
sight. There were green fields. There were
grazing grounds. There were horses,—did I
tell you that he was a horse? Oh, how I
adored him! Yes, and there were paddocks.
Dear me! It was like paradise."

She was lapsing into meditation. To set her going again, I asked,—"How old was he?"

"One year," she said, "which you know is as good as ten or twenty among you silly men."

I hardly liked ten and twenty being mixed up in this way. I was eighteen myself, and knew the difference. But there is a purpose, no doubt, of a providential kind in the superciliousness of ladies on some subjects. It may not be pleasant, but it is a natural protection against danger, like the ink of the cuttlefish.

"Yes," she went on, "he was young. I too was young, and considered very pretty. I wore my hair all fuzzy over my large brown eyes, which gave them a great deal of expression. He, too, had an unstudied carelessness about his mane and tail which became him. It was spring-time. It is generally

spring-time when a horse is one year old.
We danced."

" I understand your feelings," I murmured.

" We did not dance like you, shuffling
spinning half asleep like night owls," she
replied.   " We leaped for joy in the morning
sun.   People thought it was flies.   They were
wrong.   It was love."

" Much the same thing," I threw in ; " wings,
you know, and prickly things, and all that."

" Oh, if you are a poet !" she said, getting
up.

"No!   No!   No!" I cried hurriedly, "sit
down and go on."

She sat down rather slowly, and began
again.   " I am telling you about this for your
good.   I do not expect you to understand it
altogether, and for mercy's sake do not keep
interrupting in a silly way to show off your
appreciativeness.   It makes me nervous.
Well, as I was saying, we danced.   Ah, my

[*To face p.* 12.

HAPPY DAYS OF INNOCENCE.

poor man! If you could conceive the thrill that passed through me when his hoof touched mine——"

"What is a thrill, please?" I asked meekly.

"I wonder if I could explain it to you so that you would understand," she answered. "You see, when people don't grasp it by instinct, there is something very difficult about explaining the point of a thrill."

"Like a joke?" I suggested.

"Not at all like a joke," she snapped out. "There, you have quite upset me again. I feel like a cart of vegetables with one wheel knocked off unexpectedly. It is very trying."

"When his hoof touched yours——" I prompted, and waited for the result.

"Ah!" she sighed, "it was so strange. Yes, I think I can explain a thrill to you. You feel all of a sudden as though all your hair was blown off to the very tip of your tail, like the fluff off a dandelion, and you remain like a smooth white kid glove on a table.   And then soft warmth plays down your system, just as though the stable-cat's kitten were rubbing its head all along your back, and then——"

She stopped again.   I had dashed my hat on the ground and was holding my head with both hands.   Reason tottered on her throne.

"Well, well,—I must hurry on," she said,— "and come to the catastrophe.   We were observed."   "So were we,"—I   groaned, thinking of Violet and myself last night.

"We were observed, I stated," she continued.   "Have the goodness to attend.   Yes Mr. and Mrs. Greymare had their eye on us. They did not play fair.   They turned their backs and pretended to notice nothing."

"You have a way of saying 'yes' automatically," I noticed.   "I presume that you caught the habit in replying to young Mr. Greymare's proposals."

[*To face p.* 15.

UPLIFTED.

"You are right," she murmured,—"I did not, I could not say him nay."

Now that the whole thing returns to my mind in broad daylight, I feel a hesitation about writing that last word without a "g" and an "h" in it somewhere, but I suppose it is all right as it stands.   I am not sure what she said next.   She went off into a kind of mumbling ecstasy.   Presently I distinguished a sentence beginning "When our lips touched—ah, how we were lifted up——" and so on and so on. It was easy to see which of us was the poet, but I forbore to ask for explanations.   Mr. Colter might have been a regular Pegasus,— a sort of fly horse, for anything I could tell. As for her, I began to suspect that her con-duct had been rather light.   Of course I could see nothing, partly because there was no moon, and partly because she still wore her hair fuzzy on her forehead to give expression to her dark eyes.   But by an increased warmth in the summer air that played about us in the obscurity I knew that she was blushing.

"The next moment," she shrieked, "we were separated!"

"So were we," I groaned again, and this time she did not rebuke me. For some moments we mingled our tears in silence.

[*To face p.* 16.

THE STERN DECREE.

CHAPTER III.

" I WILL not tell you," she resumed, " the language of Mrs. Greymare. She need not have reminded me that I was beneath him. I never denied it. But there have been cases. Did I not meet a tall mule in military society whose father Cophetua was in the Stud Book, and whose mother was no better than I am? And I am told they lived very happily. Well, I suppose that it was fate. Still, I think Mr. Greymare might have done something. I glanced at him as I turned away weeping, but he never said a word. He looked sympathetic, poor soul, and I daresay his heart bled for me. Young Mr. Colter shed tears as they led him off—I know he

2

did, I found them on the common afterwards. That thistle grows on the very spot.
It is a hard world!"

"And what did they do next?" I
asked.

"What did they do? What did they not
do? ˙They bought him a groom. They
taught him paces. They took him to the
Park. They got him up as if it was Church
Parade every day. They made him look so
stiff and sour that in a year he seemed to have
lived all his life in a club. He spent hours
every day in being curry-combed, brushed,
whisped, leathered, and hand-polished before
a cheval glass. They made him think of
nothing but himself. He forgot me. He
ceased to wish to see me again. He had got
to know so much more than I. It would
have taken him a week to explain his dressing-
table to me. We were no longer equals. He
once saw me going to Covent Garden in a

[*To face p.* 18.

HOME-BRED POLISH.

[*To face p.* 19.

UNRIPE STILL.

cart. He turned away. I felt hurt so keenly that the costermonger, though prompted by kindness, was unable to distract my thoughts for an hour, until he cut his stick to a point and poked a raw place on my hind quarters. That did me good, and I was thankful to him. It is well for all of us to be restored sometimes to a true perception of the realities of life. I knew then for the first time that even costermongers were part of the Scheme of Things."

" Well—and what next?" I asked, for she had relapsed again into a silence heavy with mute emotion.

" What next?" she rasped out hoarsely, coming a step nearer. " I will tell you what next. They introduced him to an eligible young Filly !"

That was indeed hard. " And did she accept him ? "

" Not a bit, at least, not at first—in fact,

she turned up her nose at him, and told him
to go to school."

"And did he go?"

"Yes, he did ; that is, he went to what I
suppose you would call the University. But
not all at once, you know. You see the
young Filly was such a good catch that Mrs.
Greymare thought that the danger of sepa-
rating them was too great. Just as she might
be coming round, Mr. Colter might be for-
getting her at a distance, and by the time she
was ready to accept him he might be entangled
with another. But you will hardly believe it.
He fell in love with her!"

"No!"

"Yes, he did! Was it not disgraceful?
And she did nothing but snub him. At last
he took to wandering alone in the woods
weeping for her—the wicked crocodile!—and
cutting her image on a tree. They caught
him at it once. 'That boy must have

[*To face p.* 21.

"LOVE'S YOUNG DREAM."

distraction : it is preying on his mind,' said Mrs. Greymare. 'He must ; it is,' said Mr. Greymare, for he knew better than to go beyond his orders. That was the way they used to talk. Oh, *I* know them."

" Evidently you do. It is wonderful," I answered.

" Not a bit. Don't I know *you* ? "

" Yes," I replied modestly ; " but that is so easy. I am only a man."

"If so much," said the little Donkey; and I could see in the dark that she laid her ears back.

" Well," she went on, "so they walked him home and began a long speech, and the end of it all was, that if he did not go and improve his mind at once he should be treated like a foal again. They meant by that, of course, to threaten him with having his groom taken away ; and what is more, Mrs. Greymare had the impudence to say that he should be sent back to me as a punishment !"

"He was delighted, of course!"

"Not a bit of it. The nasty fickle thing had been growing up all the time from day to day, and he made a sarcastic remark about having passed the *pons assinorum*, and being ready for a University course."

"Shameful!"

"So I thought; but I have grown up myself since, and I understand him. Well, the thing was settled, and he was in good spirits again. It takes very little to put a horse in good spirits when he is good, and spirited. A man, that wants discourse of instinct, would have mourned longer."

I sighed, and fumbled in my breast for my pocket "Hamlet." She continued :—

"So Mrs. Greymare set to work to pack his box for him, because those hectoring creatures are not without motherly tendencies —it belongs to their self-importance, you know. Oh, I heard all about it from the

[To face p. 23.

MATERNAL SOLICITUDE.

servants after. There sat old Greymare in the room, pretending to read the paper, but swelling all the time with pride to think that he had actually a son going to the University. And above him hung the picture of his father in an eighteenth-century attitude, when male animals went in for what they called elegance. Beyond, on the same wall, was a photograph of Mrs. Greymare as a filly, and opposite the window hung an old painting of the Black Knight's head from King Arthur's chess board,—the ancestor of the family. Mrs. Greymare sat on the floor with the boy's box before her, putting in everything she could think of, while the young rascal stood and laughed at her."

"What did he laugh for?" I asked.

"Oh, maternal solicitude always seems a good joke to the young," replied the wise little Donkey. "I believe the fact is that she wanted to put in knee-caps, and Thorley's

food for cattle. Didn't your mother insert
mittens and jam when you went to Cambridge?"

"No, indeed; I wish she had," I replied.

"Well," said my Donkey, "I suppose not.
You are not exactly of my time, and the old
are getting so young now, and the young are
born so old, that it is really difficult to know
funny things from pathos,—or it would be, if
there were no more lovers. They are a great
comfort; they unite the two, and the difference
doesn't matter."

"Then you are not one yourself?"

"Oh, no. I am cured, you know. That is
why I am relating this. But one's heart is
never quite so blank but what the trail of the
serpent will waft o'er it still, as the poet says.
I'm not so ignorant about poets. Ah, dear
me! he has gone from me, and it is years
and years since I have heard his voice. But
even now the music of it lingers in my ears.

You would be surprised at the amount of music that can linger in my ears."

" Not at all," I replied.

There was a displeased silence for a moment. I wonder why. Could I have said anything impolite?

CHAPTER IV

" WELL, my poor man, so the young Greymare went up, as I believe they call it, and was duly admitted. I don't know the details, but at any rate he got in somehow, and went about, looking rather sheepish at first, in one of those hatchments they stick on their heads, and a sort of Inverness cape made of umbrella stuff they wear round their shoulders at the University, rain or shine."

" I beg your pardon," said I, " the cap and gown, which I suppose you are referring to, are not in the least like a hatchment and an Inverness cape."

" It is all the same to *me*," said the Donkey, with importance in her voice.

[To face p. 27.

PATERNAL ADVICE.

Perhaps she was right there.   I did not dispute the point.

" But the improving part, I am told," said the Donkey, " was when his father took leave of him in the tan-yard, or quadrangle, or whatever they call it.   He held his hoofs long and hard, and at last said in a choking voice,—

" ' Bless you, my colt !   Be good and industrious.'

" ' I will, sire,' said the young fellow."

"Did he say ' sire ' to his father ? " I asked.

" Of course," said my little friend, " colts always do."

" But I trust that it went no farther," I hinted.

" What do you mean ? " she asked innocently.

" I mean," I answered, with a little hesitation, " that I hope he did not say 'dam' to his mother."

"Oh, I daresay he did," said the Donkey;
"mares don't mind." .

She was right there. I recalled having
ridden an old mare to hounds whom I often
addressed very much that way, though I had
no hereditary right to do so. She did not
mind in the least.

"And how did the young fellow get on
at the University?" I asked.

"Very well, I believe," she answered. "He
was good and industrious. That is to say,
he was industrious that he might be good.
He chose his professors with care, and they
tell me he was soon as good with the gloves,
at any rate, as any one of his year, size, and
weight. But he went in for everything at
once. You should have seen him dive. I
was working down the towing-path at that
time, and it used to bring the tears into my
eyes. I thought it must require such courage
to dive, when one has such a very long nose.

[*To face p.* 28.

THE UNIVERSITY COURSE. NO. I.

[*To face p.* 29.

THE UNIVERSITY COURSE.   NO. II.

Fancy how the river must have flowed to his eyes, underground, so to speak! But swimming is an elegant, gentlemanly amusement. They are not always racing as they do in boats. I hate those boats. The two-year-olds so often overstrain themselves, especially in sculling. You see I know all about it. My bargee used to explain to wandering ladies on the banks, and wonder why they were so stingy not to give him drinks. Of course he did not know that it was shyness. Lots of them would have liked to have given him sixpence, only they had not the moral courage. They did not know I could read their thoughts. No more did he. He used to be disappointed, and whenever he was he used to kick me. How can men be so clumsy as to kick *forward?* The thing is absurd. I kicked him once, just to show him how. But he never got up again. I think I broke something. He was very drunk, and rolled into the river. Then I was sold back to another coster. They thought they were men. So they were. I despise men!"

"It is very kind of you to talk to me so much, in that case," I said.

"Oh, I don't mean lovers," she answered. "I told you I made an exception in their favour long ago. But I must go on telling you about my dear boy's University career. The fact was that he wanted to be perfect. He read an advertisement in a sporting paper about another colt that was not only 'reliable at water,'—he was that already, and 'handy with his feet,' the gloves made him that,—but 'clever at timber' too, so he took to cricket. I don't profess to understand cricket, though Mrs. Greymare has told me that fillies go in for it now, and donkeys will come down to it some day, for anything I can tell. They do make such a fuss all about one little ball in a big field. There is not the least reason to

[*To face p.* 30.

THE UNIVERSITY COURSE.   NO. III.

[*To face p.* 31.

run after it in the way they do. You could
knock a ton of balls that size about the same
ground, and there would be heaps of room.
And they very seldom hit each other with it.
I have seen much better fun at Covent Garden
when the costers were in good spirits, pota-
toes were cheap, and the policeman was not
looking."

"We will change the subject," said I, for
I felt myself getting angry. I am considered
a bit of a cricketer in more than one county,
and I don't look on the game as at all a fit
subject for joking.

"Well," said the Donkey, "if you like, I am
quite willing, for I don't think much more of
cricket than you do;" which was a very spite-
ful remark, if she could still read my thoughts
at all.

"There is football, now," she went on. "I
find some sense in football. Even men let out
pretty frankly there. I have seen kicks that

would not disgrace a training stable. Of course they don't kick back as they ought to, except sometimes in a crowd, but when they do !—! I used often to wish to run in and have a turn with them. It was good, I can tell you, and there cannot be the smallest doubt about its being industry. I think if he had been at the matches that old Greymare would have been pleased."

"Judging by my own experience," I ventured to say, "old Greymare would have expected his young sprig to do a little of his industry indoors. You can't take a very high position with sports only."

"That shows you don't know much about pole-jumping," she answered triumphantly. "Why, I have seen that lad take a long stick like the mast of a cutter, and run along with it held out before him as if he intended to go right through something. Then, when he got near enough to a sort of high-level

*[To face p. 32

THE UNIVERSITY COURSE.   NO. V.

[*To face p.* 33.

THE UNIVERSITY COURSE. NO. VI.

curtain-rod up in the air, like the backbone
of the roof of a house without the side ribs
and end walls, he just planted his pole in the
ground at one end, and went sailing up as the
other end rose till he popped over the roof-
bar, leaving his pole behind, and descended
like a falling star. It was lovely."

" I daresay, but you can't take a degree like
that——"

"Oh, rubbish. He could take a haystack
like that. I daresay *you* can't," she answered.

" But," I insisted, "what did he study indoors ? "

" Oh, lots : Geography, to begin with. At
least the use of the globes, I'm certain. My
bargee saw him at it once. It is an experi-
mental sort of study. There's a green table :
that represents Space. There's a rim round it :
that must be allegorical for Fate, I suppose.
Then there are gaps in the rim, and nets
beyond the gaps, which mean Accident and

Chance, or something of that kind.   Then there
is a red globe, which means the World,—or the
Soul, I don't quite know ; and two white ones,
that must be Good and Evil (one has a black
spot, the wicked one), and these two go tilting
at the red one, and very often at each other,
and sometimes they all go to the chaos
outside.   I think there is some improvement
in that study."

"Did your bargee tell you all this?"   I
asked.

"How stupid you are,—of course not!"
she said.   "You might have known it was
a Donkey's idea, if you had been paying the
smallest attention."

I begged pardon.

"But he must have studied lots more," she
went on.   "Because of the way he came out at
the exams.   "Oh yes, they have exams., just
like you, only much more sensible.   There's
the *vivâ voce* to begin with.   They do that

[To face p. 34.

THE UNIVERSITY COURSE.   NO. VII.

[*To face p.* 35.

VIVÂ VOCE EXAMINATION.

on Brighton Downs. Three examiners post
themselves at distances of a third of a mile
apart, in a row. My boy made himself heard
with perfect ease by the very furthest of them.
What do you think of that ? Full marks ? "

" I could not have done that," I answered
modestly.

" You ! ! ! " she said.

There was a long silence, during which my
wounded humility swelled up and became
very painful. I had noticed before that ladies
who are in love are not always scrupulously
careful of the feelings of persons of another
sex. Considerations of species and its limita-
tions do not always weigh with them. This
is undoubtedly an imperfection in their
characters. There is so very little, except
character, that is attractive in ladies, that im-
perfections in the character department are
peculiarly trying. I am not able to say for
certain .that they are infrequent. This is my

serious opinion.   I must press it upon Violet's
father.   I think he will recognise that I have
a decided vocation, considering my age, for
the profession of husband.

" I daresay you think that is all," she continued, when she saw that philosophy was
beginning to console me, and that the silence
did not ache quite so much.

" Doubtless," I murmured.

" You mean you don't care," she said,—
" but that is only your envy.   However, I will
tell you.   There was Free-hoof Drawing.
That is Art, if you like.   My colt could draw a
wagon and get in the shafts correctly without
even looking at it.   What do you think of
that ? "

" Full marks," I murmured,—" with the
whip," I added to myself.   I knew that she
heard my thought that time, but for some
reason or other she made no comment.   I am
sorry to say that her abstention gratified me.

[*To face p.* 36.

FREE-HOOF DRAWING EXAMINATION.

[*To face p.* 37.

NATURAL HISTORY EXAMINATION

It is strange how revengeful the best of us are. When I say the best of us, of course. I mean myself. This is not vain-glory. It is habit, like eating and drinking. They say that if you deprive a man absolutely of salt in his food he will die. I wonder if he could live if you extracted all element of conceit from his mind. I don't think he could ; I am quite sure that he ought not to. I think I will not force this opinion upon Violet's father.

"Then there was Natural History," she went on. "I helped him there. Can you imagine the question that turned the scale? It was about the natural diet of the domestic ass. No one else knew. He answered it, on paper, unmistakably. I believe I may say that his University distinctions are not without credit to me, though of course I do not claim any praise for it myself. Still, you must admit that if I had not existed at all, things would have been different. I hope you do

not consider that as going too far.   There is
nothing I dislike more than people who take
what is not their due.   I never heard any
one say that donkeys liked praise except
a German, and I think he hardly knew what
he was saying.   I know that he once made an
English friend of his very angry by clapping
him on the back and calling him a 'prig.'
He said that he meant a good square fellow
and that it was allegorical slang, as every
one knew that a prig was what you built a
house with.   So you see he meant a 'brick.'
He also says that he thinks it very foolish
of his friend to have called him a 'plastered
fool.'   I do not like to know what he meant
by that.   He writes that he has gone back to
Germany to find some one who understands
English."

[*To face p.* 39.

EDUCATION WITH HONOURS.

CHAPTER V

" AND so, to sum up," I said, having had almost as much as I could endure of this touching narrative, "your young friend carried everything before him, and came home crowned with laurels, and followed by an obsequious attendant bearing a whole tray-ful of race cups and other sporting trophies, while medals glittered on his bosom, and parchment certificates and diplomas followed by luggage train?"

"Yes! Yes, indeed!" she cried, clasping her hoofs in ecstasy at the recollection. "It is all true. Oh! they were right to tear him from me. I feel it now more than I ever did. Oh! I cannot tell you how keenly I feel it.

The truth seems to dig into me like a coster-monger."

Not having desired to produce quite such a vivid impression, I decided to control my impatience and take to the interrogative mood once more.

" And what did *you* do ? " I asked.

" I ? Oh, I acted nobly, heroically," said my poor little friend, wiping away a tear ; and added, in a plaintive voice, " Donkeys always do."

" And the old people ? " I said, to get to a less distressing part of the subject.

" Don't speak of them ! Oh, the proud, silly, puffed-up things ! " cried the little crea-ture, trembling with rage. " As if it was any merit of theirs ! And he was so good and so modest all the time, casting down his eyes and not making anything of it, while they went on with ' Bravo, *my* boy,' and ' Oh, *my* dear son,' and ' You are a colt of the old

[*To face p.* 41.

THE UNIVERSITY COURSE AT HOME.

strain!' and so on. But wait a bit. He will
be off somewhere else, one day, perhaps in
America, and they will be old, and lame, and
bony, and I shall see them in Covent Garden
with raw shoulders and no zinc ointment.
I'll let them know who I am as I go past.
I'll give them a look! They'll remember me
then. Oh, the wicked, heartless old balloons!"

We sank into silence again. Preoccupied
on her part ; prudent on mine.

Presently she began once more.

"And the worst of it was that nothing
would take them down. When the shyness
once wore off, the way in which he used to
stand with his back to the fire at home and
hold forth would have curdled the blood of
any right-minded parents. His father liked
it. I don't believe he understood three-
fourths, for he had never been a reading colt
in his youth ; an average Learned Pig at a
fair could beat him any day. But I believe

he liked the idea that his boy had got familiar
with more names than he had ever heard.
Young Colter knew the whole studbook, back
to early Egypt, and all the plates they had
run for. I think the Philosopher's plate (with
a stone in it at one time, and a cup at
another) must have been the worst of all.
They ran for it on their heads, and there was
no handicapping. There is now, though
All the entries simply start at the winning-
post and never run at all. They sit there
and read the names of the winners of former
times, and the one that reads most gets the
plate."

"Bless my soul!" I exclaimed, "what kind
of a race do they call that?"

"Education!" said the little Donkey, with
such a contemptuous snort that it withered
the grass for three yards round.

I drew myself back a few inches. Perhaps
her scorn was reasonably justifiable, but I

had sat at that winning-post reading the winners' names myself. It is strange how an unfortunate personal experience can warp our opinions on the simplest matters.

Besides which, I had a sort of vague idea that she was taking advantage of mere figures of speech as though they were arguments. That sort of thing is apt to embitter the very friendliest of relations. Sympathy between sad lovers is a pretty bond, no doubt. But if once an intrusive figure of speech comes along, and begins to make mischief, it is hard to say how long it will last.

We sulked for two precious minutes.

She made the first advances. Donkeys have so little sense of dignity.

"I did not mean to hurt your feelings, sir," she murmured, as meek as a rabbit.

I made a herculean effort to be generous.

"What can my feelings possibly be in comparison with yours?" I contrived to croak out, a little huskily, perhaps. " Please go on with your story," I added, with as desperate an attempt at cheerful interest as could be expected on such short notice.

" My story?" she said ; " oh ! it is hardly worth going on with. And besides, it is so very painful. But it is so good of you to mind. I daresay you expect what was the next thing. He actually went down by twilight, when the new moon was just above the trees, and sat outside the stable on a truss of hay by the young filly with his foreleg round her withers. The cat on the roof told me all about it. 'And he said the most beautiful things to her about the moon. I am sure I do not know where he got it from. He never used to talk about the moon to me. And the way in which he looked at her, and she looked at him, with their eyes so close the cat really thought they were trying to change eyelashes. But I hardly suppose that

[To face p. 44.

RIPE AT LAST

was really the case.   It must be a very
painful operation, and I don't think lovers
ever do anything really painful for each other
—at least, not sensible lovers.   It spoils conversation so if you are hurt.   It doesn't spoil
conversation to say the same things over
again, though ; at least, not for lovers.   And
they did that.   The cat learned every word
at last, and came and told it all to me.   I
could not help listening, though it was just
like so many stabs in my bosom.   I would
tell you all about it, but I daresay you have
done the very same, and it seems to make
you angry when *we* do the same things that
you do—I am sure I do not know why.   I
think I do not know many things.   I used
to suppose I did, but I don't."

Here she came to another stop, over-
whelmed by her own humility.   She seemed
to have a way of running into conversational
sidings, and getting brought up dead still by

a different embankment of emotion each time.
I suppose there was a want of consistency
in that, but it is very hard to say whether
consistency is such a great merit after all.
At any rate, I have always heard that when
two people feel differently, this is variety, and
everybody praises variety. The world would
be so flat without it, they say. And incon-
sistency is only one person doing the work
of two. It is variety in a nutshell.

"And so, and so,—and so," went on my
little rejected one, "that was the way. And
the old people knew all about it and never
said a word. One afternoon he and the
young filly came strolling along together in
the very field where she had seen him and
snubbed him when they were first introduced.
They were recalling it now with the greatest
satisfaction, and going over every inch of the
interview, including all the unspoken part.
It was, 'Then I said this,' and 'Then you

[*To face p.* 47.

THE UNIVERSITY COURSE JUSTIFIED.

looked that,' and 'Then I felt the other,' and
'Oh! how little I knew *then*,' and so forth."
I understood these microscopic diagrams of
automatic globules of soul invisible to the
naked heart. Love is an awful lens. When
you get time to leave off using it as a
burning-glass, and begin to peep through,
you are amazed at what you see.

"Well," went on the little one, "right in
the middle of the field sat the old people.
They looked up and saw the young lovers
coming, and Mrs. Greymare said,—'Were
we not just like that at their time of life?'
'One of us is just like that now, my love,'
he answered, looking at her in a meaning
manner. He was really a very sensible horse.
She must have led him an awful life for him
to have acquired so much judgment. Yes,
a little bird told me. The stable cat was not
there. I get to hear everything that happens,
one way or another."

" It must be most interesting," I murmured.

" Interesting !" she cried ; "oh, yes ! It is enormously interesting to be heart-broken, I assure you. It takes up all one's attention just for the time. But I was going to tell you what they did. They—I mean that wicked boy and girl—went right up to the old gentle-man, as bold as if he was a judge at an agri-cultural show, and then dropped down with a sweet smile on their knees before him. That brought things to a climax at once. Old Greymare got out his blessing and pressed it on to the tops of their heads. Mrs. Greymare got out her handkerchief and pressed it to her eyes. They really did look too silly ! I was ashamed of them. Then they all came home together, and there was such going about and exchanging calls from field to field. The hedges were made chiefly of gaps for weeks after, all through the country. It was a good thing for young Colter that he had practised

[*To face p.* 48.

"BLESS YOU, MY CHILDREN!"

casting down his eyes and looking uncom-
fortable when he came back in all his glory
from' the university. It made some sort of a
lead for him, for he had to follow himself in
the same line now—the only difference that
it was genuine this time. He did feel foolish.
He knew at the bottom of his heart that he
was being shown off as a kind of new orna-
ment that the young filly had got to wear.
The married horses used to give him an eye
now and then from under their forelocks, and
just lay back one ear playfully for a moment.
They knew the whole staircase of which he
had got his foot on the first step. They knew
the extraordinary and paradoxical nature of
its architecture too, for whereas man and wife
tread it together in step, such is the con-
struction of the ladder that one goes up-
stairs and one goes downstairs for ever and
ever."

"May I ask," I interrupted, with some

4

hesitation, " where you learned to speak so nicely about all this ? "

" From an owl," replied my Donkey, rather shortly. Then she continued, " But the excitement began when the presents came pouring in. There were three hundred and seventy-nine of them. A magpie, who is taking care of the portable ones in an old oak tree, counted them for me. There was not at first such variety as you would suppose. Some people sent complete sets of harness, Munster clothing for indoors, surcingles, pillar-reins, and so forth. The greater number sent shoes. If they had been straightened out a light railway could have been made of them. Lots of these were in silver, much too good for every-day use. Some were plated, which is silly, for after a single gallop the plating wears off and shows the copper, and then, for the life of you, you dare not lift up your heels for fear of being caught. And then the nails !

Some had fancy heads. Some were steel. Some were patent screws. Some were mere wooden pegs. Some—I am ashamed to say— had been used before, and were cleaned and beaten out for the occasion. Most were of the usual kind. There were ten pails full of them. The pails came separately. So did the wheelbarrow from a royal stable. That young filly went wheeling it about all day, and tilting it up to show the monogram. Really, I have no patience to tell you of all the things they had."

I could not but feel flattered, in the short pause that she made here to collect her re- miniscences, to see that at least my little friend had no doubt about the patience of her listener. I think I had deserved this, but the flattery we get from ladies is more apt to be of free gift, election, and grace, than works.

In the innocence of my heart I supposed

we had got to the end of the subject of the presents. I should know better now, but I was not married then, and the action of the feminine mind still had its mysteries for me. I was soon undeceived.

"Yes,"—said the little one, just as though I had spoken,—"I think those nails gave more trouble than all the rest. There were so many of them, you see, and the greater part had no maker's name or any sign on the parcel to say where one could go afterwards and change them at a loss for something useful. And there is always a certain amount of danger in advertising them in a paper, like 'The Lady Mare,' for instance. People are so sharp at catching that sort of thing, and one never knows what they read. Besides, arrangements had to be made that the actual exchange was not to come off till after the ceremony, because a lot of the givers would be there looking out for their presents, which

quite filled a loose box and two stalls. If
some female relation had missed hers, there
would have been a family quarrel that might
have injured the prospects of the foals,—if
any.   There was just one nail that the young
filly would not have parted with at any
price, for she was not absolutely heartless, after
all.   That had belonged to a poor spavined
old thing that had drawn a cart in the same
farm, and went limping round and round now
in a brick-crushing machine.   She pulled it
out of her cracked foot with her own teeth,
for she could not afford to buy one, and
was too proud to beg.   The consequence was
that the shoe came half off, and a workman
who had never been in a blacksmith's office
in his life hammered in a great house-nail
instead, and it went to the wrong place, and
gave more pain to the wretched thing than if
he had run it into her eye.   She had to limp
and groan for three weeks after, and never

said a word. It is a very touching story,
isn't it? You don't often hear of that sort of
devotion among the humans, do you?"

I was certainly not prepared with a case on
all fours with it from members of my own
species. The story went on :—

"Well,—I suppose, being a man, you can
hardly be expected to know enough to understand all about these things, so I will just tell
you in two words that the ceremony was
simply splendid. The bride looked lovely,
with her mane all frizzed and filled with
white clover flowers. She had to roll in them
from eight o'clock in the morning till ten, and
then keep quite still to prevent their falling
out before the breakfast. Her white coat
shone like satin, and she was followed to the
paddock by six young strawberry roans,
walking two and two like a circus. Her
father gave her away. He was an old
charger from the Scots Greys, and looked

very grand and military, especially about the
nose. Poor young Colter was as nervous
as if he had never been to college, and if his
Best Horse had not given him a nudge and
whispered to remember his triumph in the
vivâ voce examination, he would never have
brought out a sound. When it was over they
all sat down to bran mash with beer in it,
and you ought just to have seen the cutting
of the Thorley's food cake. I cried, I do
assure you, but not with envy. Still, I could
not help thinking what it would have been
like if I had been in *her* place. And they
do say that it need not have been such an
unequal match after all, for though I could
never become what he was, if he had married
me he would certainly have been what I am,
and equality is everything in married life.

"There was a noble speech from the old
trooper full of beautiful thoughts. I wish I
could remember it for you."

" Please do not," I gasped faintly.

"Oh, you would admire it, I know. It was
all about keeping neck and neck through the
race of life, and remembering not to expect
it to be all on the flat, but preparing the mind
for the steeplechase course that it really was,
and never swerving at the five-barred gate of
difficulty, or jumping short at the waters of
affliction, and doing all this so as to keep in
condition for greater things in case your
country needed you ; and when the trumpet
for the last great charge should sound——
but I cried so much I really can't remember
it all."

" Please do not distress yourself," I murmured.

" And I'll tell you what I did !" she suddenly began again, with a last dash of cheer-
fulness. " Just as they drove away I suddenly
remembered that there were some old shoes
nailed inside the barn door. And I got in

[*To face p.* 57.

MAGNANIMITY.

and scrambled over the straw anyhow, and
hooked one down and sent it flying after them
like a quoit. I do hope it will bring them
good luck. At any rate, it only just escaped
breaking both their necks, and that is always
something at a wedding. Well—well—well
—so it is past, and my little dream of life
is done. I am very glad to have had this
opportunity of telling you all about it, and I
sincerely hope it will have done you good."

At this moment the clock struck one. The
charm was over. I started to my feet. I
was alone. A sound of retreating steps and
a dim form jogging away, with long ears
flapping in the darkness, assured me that I
had, at least, been not entirely victimised by
hallucination.

How far the whole incident was a little
dream of my own I really cannot say. I
should like to go down to the common again
at the same witching hour and try once more,

but times are changed. I have been through
the dread experience of young Colter Greymare myself now, and I am expected to be
in when I ought to be, and if I am out late
it is no longer in an irresponsible manner
like a stray sheep, but with a white shirt in
front and a black coat on my back, and the
coachman ordered at a pre-arranged moment
to take me—no, I should have said to take
us—home.

Still, it may do some one else good—who
knows?   Here it is, at any rate, on the
chance.

THE END.

Printed by Hazell, Watson, & Viney, Ld., London and Aylesbury.

PUBLICATIONS

OF

GEORGE ALLEN.

BY *AUGUSTUS J. C. HARE.*

NORTH-EASTERN FRANCE.

1 vol., crown 8vo, cloth, 10s. 6d.   With Map and 86
Woodcuts.   532 pages.

Picardy—Abbeville and Amiens—Paris and its Environs—Arras
and the Manufacturing Towns of the North—Champagne—Nancy
and the Vosges, etc.

SOUTH-EASTERN FRANCE.

1 vol., crown 8vo, cloth, 10s. 6d.   With Map and 176
Woodcuts.   600 pages.

The different Lines to the South—Burgundy—Auvergne—The
Cantal—Provence—The Alpes Dauphinaises and Alpes Maritimes,
etc.

SOUTH-WESTERN FRANCE.

1 vol., crown 8vo, cloth, 10s. 6d.   With Map and 232
Woodcuts.   664 pages.

The Loire—The Gironde and Landes—Creuse—Corrèze—The
Limousin—Gascoiny and Languedoc—The Cevennes and the
Pyrenees, etc.

London : GEORGE ALLEN, 8, Bell Yard, Temple Bar ; and
Sunnyside, Orpington.

THE WEB OF LIFE.

Crown 8vo, cloth, 6s.

"When so many novels have a cynical flavour, it is a great pleasure to be able to recommend one which touches a good many of the sore places of our social system, and yet breathes throughout a spirit of charity to all classes."—*Guardian*, September 25, 1889.

"A clever and thoughtful book . . . decidedly above the average; and it is suggestive as well as interesting."—*Graphic*, October 26, 1889.

"No one could wish a prettier bit of reading for holiday hours."—*Literary World*, September 20, 1889.

THEY HAVE THEIR REWARD.

Crown 8vo, cloth, 6s.

"Miss Atkinson is to be congratulated upon having added a genuinely original touch of romance to the familiar miser of fiction."—*Athenæum*, May 17, 1890.

"We are ready to take a good deal for granted, if the personages of a story really interest us, as they certainly do in Miss Atkinson's story."—*Spectator*, August 23, 1890.

"The promise furnished by 'The Web of Life' is here fulfilled. There pervades it, from first to last, an earnest moral purpose."—*Liverpool Mercury*, May 7, 1890.

"It is not a commonplace story, and treats some important questions with a freshness and originality that are very attractive."—*Sheffield Independent*, May 10, 1890.

"We have not come across a better all-round book than this for a long time."—*Church Review*, October 3, 1890.

London : GEORGE ALLEN, 8, Bell Yard, Temple Bar ; and Sunnyside, Orpington.

BY REV. BASIL EDWARDS, M.A.,

Late of Gonville and Caius College, Cambridge; Rector of
Ashleworth, Gloucester.

SONGS OF A PARISH PRIEST.

*With Full-page Woodcut of Old Churchyard Cross at Ashle-
worth, and Music to " Our Mother Church of England."*

In Parchment Wrapper, 2s.; cloth, 2s. 6d.; roan, gilt edges,
4s. 6d.   Second Edition.

EXTRACT FROM PREFACE.

"It has seemed to the writer of this little book, that in
every parish and every country village there are, besides the
living voice of the Church, numberless silent witnesses which
appeal to her sons' and daughters' hearts; and that all the
associations, even of the material things which form part of
and surround the 'houses of God in the land,' are intensely
sacred, and are full of teaching.   The quiet of a country
charge has enabled the writer to endeavour to link together
many of the objects most prominently connected with sacred
thought in a rural parish, and to present the results to the
reader in somewhat of a sequence, leading step by step from
the Lych-Gate to the Altar."

"They seem to me singularly attractive, both in grace of com-
position and in spirit and thought.   I have not often been so much
touched and satisfied by sacred poetry.   It is a gift to us all,
for which I am grateful.—Yours faithfully, R. W. CHURCH.   The
Deanery, St. Paul's, August 10, 1888."

London: GEORGE ALLEN, 8, Bell Yard, Temple Bar; and
Sunnyside, Orpington.

4